W9-BHU-818

Enchanting Classics

for Children

Illustrated by Tony Wolf
Adapted by Clementina Coppini
and Louise Gikow

From the works of:
Alexandre Dumas, Jules Verne,
R.L. Stevenson, and Howard Pyle

★ A Tell-Me-A-Story Keepsake Treasury ★

Enchanting Classics
for Children

Dalmatian Press

ENCHANTING CLASSICS *for* CHILDREN
Copyright © 2004 Dami International, Milano

All rights reserved
Printed in China

Cover Design: Emily Robertson

Published in 2004 by Dalmatian Press, LLC.
The DALMATIAN PRESS name and logo are trademarks
of Dalmatian Press, LLC, Franklin, Tennessee 37067.
No part of this book may be reproduced or copied in any form
without the written permission of Dalmatian Press.

ISBN: 1-40370-790-1
13340-0504

04 05 06 07 SFO 10 9 8 7 6 5 4 3 2 1

Tell Me A Story.

When you read a story to your child, lots of good things happen. You show your child that reading is exciting and fun. You encourage the growth and development not just of your little one's imagination but also his or her vocabulary, comprehension skills, and overall school readiness.

Research shows, time and time again, that children who are read to on a regular basis do significantly better in school than children who are not read to at home. We encourage you to spend ten to twenty minutes every day reading to your child. It's a small amount of quality time that reaps a big reward!

It's also important to keep reading books *to* your child and *with* your child even after he or she is reading independently. You can share books that are slightly more difficult than what your child is reading on his or her own because you are available to help with vocabulary words and any questions your child may have about the story.

Read and Discuss.

No matter how old your child is, or how well she is reading independently, remember that story time is the perfect opportunity to talk about what you're reading and any other topics that might arise from it. This kind of dialog helps make stories come alive and adds depth to your child's reading experience.

What would you do if you were in the story? you might ask. *How might you fix this problem? Did the character do the right thing?* and so forth.

Your child's Keepsake Treasury includes dialogic questions throughout the stories to prompt meaningful and memorable conversations. Ask your own questions as well. You might be surprised at the imaginative discussions that follow. You can learn more about dialogic reading online at: *http://www.readingrockets.org.*

We hope that *Enchanting Classics for Children* will become a treasured part of your family's library.

Happy Reading!

CONTENTS

THE THREE MUSKETEERS

Adapted from the story by Alexandre Dumas

When I was a young man, my father gave me an old horse. Then he sent me out into the world to seek my fortune.

I wanted to be a musketeer. The musketeers are special soldiers who guard the king of France.

My name is D'Artagnan.

And this is my story.

I rode my horse for a long time. Finally, I came to an inn. There, I met a strange man. He had a scar under his eye.

He told me my horse looked silly. He told me *I* looked silly.

I challenged him to a duel. But instead, his servants attacked me.

The next morning, when I got up, I saw the strange man again.

He was talking to a beautiful lady. He called her "Milady."

"My name is D'Artagnan," I told him. "And the next time I see you, I will defeat you!"

When I got to Paris, I went to visit my father's friend, Mr. Treville. He was going to help me become a musketeer.

On my way out, I accidentally bumped into a musketeer.

"Watch where you're going!" he said rudely.

Then he gruffly challenged me to a duel.

"I will meet you tomorrow," I told him. "My name is D'Artagnan."

"I am Athos," he said.

Just after that, I bumped into another musketeer.

His name was Porthos. He also challenged me to a duel.

I had been in Paris for one hour, and already I was to fight two duels!

Then I saw a handkerchief. It belonged to a third musketeer. I picked it up with my sword and gave it back to him.

"You have ripped it," he told me.

"It was ripped before I picked it up!" I said.

He shook his head. "My name is Aramis, and I challenge you to a duel."

"I'll be there," I told him.

The next morning, I went to meet the three musketeers.

"There he is," said Athos, pointing to me. "I am to fight a duel with him."

"No, I am," said Porthos.

"No, I am!" said Aramis.

They looked at one another and laughed.

"You must be a very brave man," Aramis told me, "to fight three musketeers in one day."

Just then, a group of soldiers arrived. "Who are they?" I asked.

"They work for the Cardinal Richelieu," said Athos. "They are our worst enemies!"

The cardinal worked for the king. But he was a bad man. He wanted power. He wanted to tell the king exactly what to do.

So the musketeers were always fighting with his soldiers.

"There are many of them, and only three of us!" said Porthos.

"There are four of us," I said and I began to fight.

Aramis smiled.

The battle was long, but we won.

When it was over, Aramis said, "You fought well, D'Artagnan."

And from that day on, I was not alone. I had three new friends—Athos, Porthos, and Aramis.

D'Artagnan has made three new friends. Who are your best friends?

Soon after, I was sent for by king Louis of France.

He wanted to meet the young man who had helped the three musketeers.

The king's musketeers were not supposed to fight—especially with the cardinal's soldiers. But when they fought for the king, he was secretly pleased. He knew that the cardinal could not be trusted.

"You are a brave young man," he told me.

I couldn't wait to leave the palace. I wanted to tell Athos, Porthos, and Aramis that I had seen the king!

"If the king likes you, he will surely make you a musketeer," Aramis told me.

But before I could become a musketeer, I had to go to a special school.

My friends cheered for me and the other cadets as we walked through the streets of Paris.

I might not have been a real musketeer yet, but I would be someday.

And in the meantime, I had three musketeer friends—Athos, Porthos, and Aramis!

Athos was a gentleman. He was very elegant and had good manners.

Porthos spent all of his money on good food and expensive clothes.

Aramis was the most handsome. He loved books and reading.

They were all very different. But they were all very brave.

And they were all loyal to the king.

Do you have friends who are different from you? Who are they? How are they different?

In Paris, I rented a room from a baker named Monsieur Bonacieux. He lived there with his daughter, Constance. She was a lady-in-waiting to Queen Anne, and she was very pretty.

One day, I came home to find Monsieur Bonacieux in tears. "Look!" he exclaimed, handing me a letter.

We have kidnapped your daughter, the letter read. *If you don't want anything to happen to her, don't search for her.*

"Do you have any suspects?" I asked.

"For the last few days, a strange man with a scar has been following her," he told me. "And I just saw him a few minutes ago!"

"A man with a scar?" I cried. "I met a man with a scar! His servants beat me! And I have vowed to have my revenge!"

I ran out in search of my enemy. But I didn't find him. And when I returned home, Monsieur Bonacieux was gone, too.

"The cardinal's guards arrested him," a neighbor told me.

I wondered. Could the man with the scar be working for the cardinal?

The next morning, I heard noises coming from downstairs. I lay down and put my ear to the floor.

"Go away! Leave me alone!" a woman's voice cried.

In an instant, I rushed down the stairs.

A young woman sat on a chair surrounded by a group of men. It was Constance!

I pulled out my sword and challenged the men.

After a short battle, they ran away.

Later that day, I went to see my friends, Athos, Porthos, and Aramis. I told them what Constance had told me.

"Constance works for the queen," I explained. "She was kidnapped, but she escaped. Then, her father was arrested. She needs our help. The queen needs our help."

My friends needed to hear no more. If it was for the queen, they would do it.

"We must take the oath of the musketeers!" Aramis said. All three stood up and crossed their swords. They asked me to do the same.

"All for one and one for all!" cried Athos.

"All for one and one for all!" we all said.

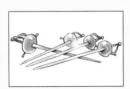

What do you think that means, "all for one and one for all"?

When I returned home, I saw two figures slip away into the darkness. One of them was Constance!

I followed them to the palace.

"Shhh!" said Constance when she saw me. "This is the Duke of Buckingham, from England. He is here to see my mistress, Queen Anne. They are good friends.

"But the king is very jealous," Constance went on. "And Cardinal Richelieu is always spying on us. I fear something terrible will happen!"

The king had given Queen Anne twelve beautiful diamond brooches. That night, Queen Anne gave them to the duke. She did this because she wanted peace between France and England.

The problem was, the cardinal's spies saw the queen give the brooches to the duke. And this didn't fit in with his plans.

France and England were always fighting. And the cardinal liked it that way. When the two countries fought, the cardinal had more power. The king was weak, and he let the cardinal control his army.

"The king listens to the queen. He will not fight England," the cardinal thought. "But what if he were to find out that the queen had given her diamond jewelry to a young, handsome Englishman? Then perhaps he would listen to me! All I need is a spy to watch the queen… and a thief to steal the diamonds!"

The cardinal sent for Monsieur Bonacieux.

"I am innocent," Bonacieux told him. "I don't know why I was arrested."

"Do not worry," the cardinal said. "You are free. And take this gold. I am very sorry."

"Thank you," replied Bonacieux. "Is there anything I can do for you?"

"You can keep an eye on your daughter, Constance, for me," Cardinal Richelieu said.

"Certainly," said Bonacieux, bowing to the cardinal.

Richelieu had his spy. Now he needed a thief.

He called for Rochefort, his right-hand man… Rochefort, who had a scar under his eye!

"Take this letter to Milady," he told Rochefort.

The letter said: *Buckingham has twelve diamond brooches, given to him by the Queen of France. Steal two of them and bring them to me. You will be rewarded.*

Milady was a friend of the cardinal. And she was the best thief in Paris.

She had no trouble stealing the diamonds.

When Richelieu had the two diamond brooches, he went to see the king.

"Sire, what do you think about organizing a ball?" he asked. "It would make the queen very happy!"

"What a good idea!" exclaimed king Louis. "It's been a long time since we have had a celebration at the palace."

The cardinal then said, "You must ask the queen to wear the twelve diamond brooches that you gave her for her birthday."

"Another good idea!" the king said. And that's exactly what he did.

"Will you wear the diamonds?" he asked Queen Anne.

"Gladly!" she said.

Oh, no! The king wants Queen Anne to wear the diamond brooches. But the Duke of Buckingham has them. What do you think Queen Anne will do?

The queen was worried. If she did not wear the diamond brooches, the king would be very angry.

"I must send a letter to the Duke of Buckingham in London. He must return the diamonds to me," she told Constance.

"I know four men who would do anything for you," Constance told her. "D'Artagnan and his three musketeer friends will help us."

So the queen gave Constance the letter, and she gave it to me. But we needed money for the trip.

Constance begged her father for some gold. "I need it to go to London!" she told him.

But he refused. So she opened his safe and took the gold anyway.

Up in my room, we heard noises. We took out a tile in the floor so we could see what was going on downstairs.

A strange man sat with Bonacieux.

"Constance wanted money," Bonacieux told him. "She talked about going to London to take care of something for the queen."

Bonacieux was spying for the stranger!

Then I recognized him.

"The man with the scar!" I gasped.

But there was no time to challenge him now. I had to go to London for the queen!

Athos, Porthos, Aramis, and I started for London right away.

We were headed for the town of Calais. There, we would find a boat and sail to England.

When we were halfway there, Porthos stopped.

"I'm hungry and thirsty," he told us. "I need something to eat and drink."

So we went to an inn.

But after the meal, a man insulted Porthos. "I must stay and fight him," Porthos cried. "You go on ahead."

We rode some more.

Then we were attacked by robbers, and Aramis was wounded.

"Don't worry, D'Artagnan!" Athos cried. "I'll hold them off. You go on to London!"

By now, I was sure that someone was trying to stop us from getting to London. So I went on alone.

Soon I arrived at Calais, where a boat was leaving for England.

As I sailed away, I thought of my friends. I hoped they were all right!

Do you think Athos, Porthos, and Aramis are all right? What do you think happened to them?

I soon landed in England. When I reached the Duke of Buckingham's palace, I gave him the letter from Queen Anne. "It's a matter of life or death," I told him.

"I will return the diamond brooches to you immediately," he said. But when he went to get them, he discovered something terrible.

"Two of them are missing!" he cried. "They must have been stolen! And I know exactly who did it. It was the thief—Milady! Cardinal Richelieu must have ordered her to steal them!"

"What are we to do?" I asked.

"I know," Buckingham said.

He called for a jeweler. We waited all day and all night as the jeweler made two more diamond brooches. They matched the first ten perfectly!

"Now take them to the queen," the Duke of Buckingham told me. "And good luck!"

A few days later, I arrived in Paris. When I entered the city, there were carriages everywhere! It was the evening of the Great Ball.

I rushed to the palace and returned the diamond brooches to the queen.

"Oh, thank you!" she cried. "You have saved me… and France!"

While I had been racing toward the queen, the cardinal went to see the king.

"I'm sorry to tell you this," he said. He handed a box to the king. "The queen gave these brooches to the Duke of Buckingham. Perhaps she loves England more than she loves France."

The king was very angry and jealous.

Just then, the queen entered the room. She was wearing the diamond brooches!

"Count them!" hissed the cardinal. "See if all twelve are there."

The king tried. But the music started. And everyone began to dance.

After the dance was over, the king gave the box with the two diamond brooches to the queen.

"Here are your missing brooches," he declared.

"But your Majesty," Queen Anne replied gaily, "I am not missing any brooches. I am wearing all twelve!"

The king counted them… and she was!

"What is going on?" the king asked Richelieu.

"I… I… I wanted to give the queen a gift," Cardinal Richelieu lied.

"Thank you," said Queen Anne, smiling at the cardinal. "You are very kind."

How do you think the queen feels about the cardinal now? Do you think she trusts him?

But she knew the truth—Richelieu had tried to betray her.

Only the king was fooled.

I had saved the queen's honor!

The following morning, I left Paris to find my friends.

On my way, I saw the beautiful woman again... the one who had been talking to the man with the scar.

"I am Lady Clarick, but everyone calls me Milady," she told me. She was English, but spoke perfect French. "You must visit me in Paris."

So this was the Milady who had stolen the diamonds! And she was friendly with the man with the scar!

I would watch out for her...

I soon found Athos, Porthos, and Aramis. They had all been wounded on our race to England. But they were better now.

However, Constance had disappeared.

I knew Milady was mixed up in all this.

So I decided to find out what was going on.

Milady invited me to dine with her, and I accepted. She seemed to like me.

After dinner, rather than going home, I secretly hid in a closet. I wanted to see what she would do next.

I heard Milady talking to herself as she looked in the mirror.

"I hate that D'Artagnan," she said. "He made me look bad. Now the cardinal doesn't believe that I stole the diamonds at all! Well, I'll make D'Artagnan pay..."

I jumped from the closet.

"So it *was* you who stole the queen's diamonds!" I cried.

"Help!" Milady called for her guards. "There is a man in my room!"

I needed to escape. But how?

I grabbed a dress, a cape, and a bonnet and put them on over my uniform.

It wasn't a great disguise, but it was better than nothing.

Then I ran for my life.

> *If you could disguise yourself as someone*
> *or something, who or what would it be?*

Finally, I reached
Athos's house.

"You can't go to war
dressed like that!"
Athos laughed.

"War? What war?" I asked.

"England has attacked us at the town of La Rochelle," Athos told me. "Here. Try on this uniform."

The uniform fit perfectly. And soon, Athos, Porthos, Aramis, and I were marching with the King of France. We were riding to defend our country!

It was a fierce battle. And we were winning.

That night my friends and I stayed at an inn. Through a pipe in the wall, we heard Cardinal Richelieu come in.

"Shhh!" Athos said. "Let's hear what the cardinal has to say!"

The cardinal was talking to Milady.

"Milady," he said. "You must find a way to get rid of the Duke of Buckingham."

"In return," Milady said, "I want D'Artagnan in prison… for life!"

"Very well," said the cardinal. And he gave her a letter that allowed Milady to do whatever she wanted. It was signed: *Cardinal Richelieu.*

"That letter is dangerous!" Aramis whispered. "It gives Milady too much power!"

"Leave it to me," said Athos.

That night, he secretly took the letter from Milady's pocket. Then he gave it to me.

The next day, we had to fight again. And as we fought, we talked. We decided to write two letters of our own.

The first one was to Queen Anne. We told her of the cardinal's plans.

The second was to the Duke of Buckingham. Even though he was our enemy, we knew he wanted peace.

We told him to watch for the cardinal's spies. We especially warned him about Milady.

Luckily, they both got the letters in time.

The cardinal then sent Rochefort—the man with the scar—to arrest *us*. He wanted his revenge.

But I still had the letter the cardinal had given Milady.

It said: *Whatever this person does is done for the well-being of France*! And of course, it was signed by the cardinal himself!

So Rochefort could not arrest us. We were saved!

Cardinal Richelieu was defeated. Much to my surprise, he decided to make me a musketeer anyway.

"Congratulations!" said Porthos. "Now you are one of us!"

I put on the uniform of the musketeers. It fit perfectly!

D'Artagnan is very proud to be a musketeer. What makes you proud?

Then Athos, Porthos, Aramis, and I went out to celebrate.
"All for one, and one for all!" we shouted.
I was truly a musketeer at last!

AROUND THE WORLD IN EIGHTY DAYS

Adapted from the story by Jules Verne

My name is Passepartout.

I have had many jobs. I have worked in a circus. I have worked as a butler. I have traveled the world and have had many exciting adventures. But none were as exciting as the adventures I was about to have with my new employer…

I had finally decided to settle down. So I got a job in London with an English gentleman named Mr. Phileas Fogg.

Mr. Fogg liked peace and quiet and order. He was always on time. So when Mr. Fogg hired me, I thought it would be an easy job.

But I was wrong.

Mr. Fogg belonged to a club called the Reform Club. There, he played cards with four friends. They were the engineer, Andrew Stuart, and three bankers—John Sullivan, Samuel Fallentin, and Thomas Flanagan.

On the day Mr. Fogg hired me, there had been a robbery at the Bank of England. The director of the bank, Gauthier Ralph, was talking to them.

"The thief dressed and acted like a gentleman," Ralph said, shaking his head.

"You will never catch him, I'm afraid," said Stuart. "The world is a very big place."

"Not so very big," said Mr. Fogg. "Somewhere, I read that you could make a complete trip around the world in eighty days."

"That's impossible!" said Flanagan.

"I could do it," said Fogg.

"I bet five thousand pounds that you can't!" cried Flanagan.

———❖———

Fogg came home a little before eight.

"In ten minutes we have to be at the station," he told me. "We are going to travel around the world in eighty days."

I nearly fainted with surprise.

I packed Mr. Fogg's bags. He gave me a lot of money to bring on the trip.

 Do you think Mr. Fogg will be able to win the bet?

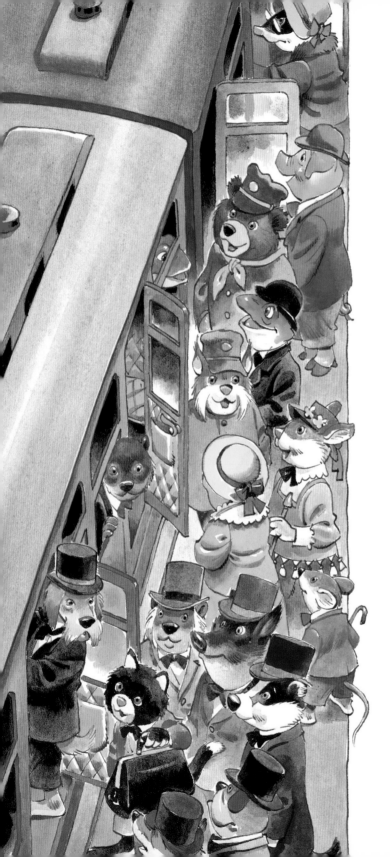

At the station, Mr. Fogg gave some money to a poor woman. I was glad to see he was a generous person.

Then we boarded the train.

Mr. Fogg's friends from the Reform Club were there to see us off.

"Have a good trip. And remember, you must be back in eighty days!" they said to Fogg as the train pulled away.

"Yes," said Mr. Fogg, consulting his watch. "I will be back on Saturday, December 21st, 1872, at 8:45 P.M."

It was the second of October.

One week later, we reached Suez, Egypt.

On the wharf was a man in a checked suit and hat. His name was Inspector Fix.

Fix was a detective. He was searching for the man who had robbed the Bank of England.

Inspector Fix followed me to the bazaar. I had gone there to buy some things for our trip.

He was friendly, and so I told him about Mr. Fogg's bet. I even told him about all the money I was carrying. He seemed very interested.

Why do you think Inspector Fix is interested in Mr. Fogg's money? Can you guess?

Next, Mr. Fogg and I took a ship, the *Mongolia*, to India. Inspector Fix was also on board. Soon, we reached Bombay. From there, we took a train.

After only a day, the train stopped. "There are no more train tracks!" the conductor explained. "They haven't been built yet!"

What were we to do? If we didn't keep going, we would lose precious time!

Mr. Fogg left us for a moment. Then he came back... with an elephant!

"Let's go, Passepartout!" he told me.

An Englishman, Sir Francis Cromarty, came with us.

That night, we camped in the forest. Suddenly, a group of people dressed in exquisite, colorful clothing appeared. Behind a carriage walked a beautiful young woman held by armed guards.

"What is going on?" I asked.

"The Raja of Bundelkhand has died," Cromarty explained. "His body will be burned. The young woman is his wife, the Princess of Bundelkhand. According to tradition, she must be burned with him."

"But we must rescue her!" insisted Fogg.

"You cannot!" Cromarty said, grabbing Fogg's arm. "They will harm you, too!"

But I had an idea…

> *What would you do to save the princess?*

The fire had been lit. The air was full of smoke.

Quickly, I used my shirt to make a turban, so that I could look like the other people.

Then I climbed onto the platform and lifted the young woman up.

The crowd thought I was a ghost. They just stood there in amazement as I vanished with the princess.

"We must hurry!" I whispered to my friends as soon as I got back to our camp.

We escaped just in time!

"You were very brave, Passepartout," said Mr. Fogg.

The princess's name was Aouda. We were happy to have her travel with us.

We soon reached Calcutta.

But there, Mr. Fogg and I were both arrested!

We were told it was because I had entered a forbidden Hindu temple.

It delayed us for three days. But finally, we were let out of jail. Princess Aouda was waiting for us.

A few hours later, we were on a boat to Hong Kong.

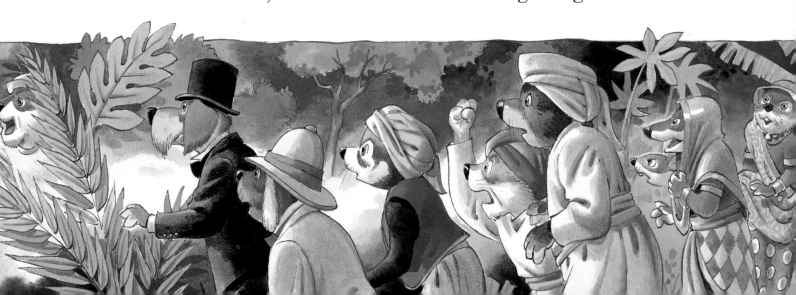

On the way to Hong Kong, we stopped in the city of Singapore. There, we rode on a rickshaw.

Mr. Fogg wanted to show Princess Aouda the city. I left them to walk around.

"When you are done, come back to the hotel," Mr. Fogg told me. "Our ship is leaving early tomorrow."

Singapore was very crowded. It was full of houses, stores, and interesting things to see. I was happy to have some time to relax and look around a bit.

But while I was looking around, whom should I see... ...but Inspector Fix!

I was beginning to be suspicious. Was he following us?

Sure enough—he was! And he told me why.

"I am sure your employer, Phileas Fogg, was the very man who robbed the Bank of England!" he said. "And I need your help to capture him."

"I will not help you," I told him. "My employer is a gentleman. He could not be a thief."

But Mr. Fix managed to delay me. I missed the boat to Hong Kong!

I was alone in Singapore. Mr. Fogg was far away. What was I to do?

How can you tell that Passpartout is a loyal friend to Mr. Fogg?

I managed to find another ship, and I ended up in Yokohama, Japan.

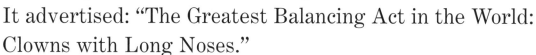

But I had no money with me.

I had to find a job.

Luckily, I saw a man with a sign. It advertised: "The Greatest Balancing Act in the World: Clowns with Long Noses."

Since I had been an acrobat in my youth, I became a clown with a long nose. In the act, I would be a part of a great human pyramid.

That night, during the very last act, I saw Mr. Fogg in the audience! I was so excited that I ran off the stage. The pyramid tumbled to the ground behind me.

But I had found my employer again.

"We must go quickly," Mr. Fogg said. "The *General Grant* is waiting to take us to America."

"Who is that?" I asked.

"It is a ship," he explained. "We must leave right away."

"How did you get to Yokohama?" I asked Mr. Fogg when we were aboard.

"We were waiting for you, so we missed the sailing of the *Carnatic*," he explained. "But luckily, we met a sailor who let us travel with him."

"He suggested to us that we go to Yokohama, where he was headed," Aouda added. "From Yokohama, we could take the *General Grant* to America."

"How lucky for me!" I exclaimed.

"There was a terrible storm on the way," Aouda went on. "But Mr. Fogg was very brave. And a nice Englishman traveled with us."

"What was his name?" I asked suspiciously.

"Mr. Fix," she said.

Oh, no! I thought. *Inspector Fix is still following us!*

The *General Grant* sailed to America. I often saw Inspector Fix on deck.

There was nothing he could do to us, however. He could not arrest us in America. He had to wait until Mr. Fogg got back to England.

There was nothing I could do, either…

…except wait.

Eventually, we arrived in San Francisco. It was December 3rd. We were exactly on schedule!

We were going to cross America by train. But our train didn't leave for a few hours. So we decided to take a walk.

San Francisco was a lively city. We found ourselves in the middle of a political rally. It was very exciting.

But then, a man bumped into Aouda. His name was Colonel Proctor, and he wasn't very nice.

Mr. Fix tried to defend her, but Colonel Proctor threw him to the ground. Then he challenged Mr. Fogg to a duel!

But luckily, there was no time.

We quickly boarded the carriage that took us to the train.

It was time to go!

It would take us a week to travel by train from San Francisco to New York. From there, we could board a ship for England.

One morning, I was looking out of the train window when I saw a giant cloud of dust on the horizon.

It was a large herd of buffalo!

They were moving closer and closer. Soon, they started to cross the train tracks. We were forced to stop for hours, waiting for all of the buffalo to pass by.

Unfortunately, that was when we discovered that Colonel Proctor was on the train.

Once again, he challenged Mr. Fogg to a duel.

Mr. Fogg accepted.

"Please be careful!" Aouda begged.

But the two never had their duel... because just then, we were attacked by a group of American Indians!

We all fought bravely, including Aouda.

But while I was fighting, I was knocked over the head and fell off the train.

I was captured and held for many hours. Suddenly, some soldiers arrived and freed me. At their head was Mr. Fogg!

He had rescued me! But we had lost valuable time.

When we got to the train station, Aouda and Fix were waiting for us. But our train had left the station. To make matters worse, a blizzard blew in.

"Oh, no!" I cried. "If it had not been for me, you would have caught the train. It's all my fault!"

Mr. Fogg sat and reflected on what to do. We were twenty hours behind schedule. Who knew when another train would come by!

Suddenly, Fix said, "I know how we can catch up with the train!"

I thought he was trying to delay us, though I couldn't imagine why. But his idea was actually a good one.

He had noticed a sled with a sail attached to it. So, using the force of the wind, we slipped along on the snow for many miles.

Finally, we caught up with the train again.

But there was more bad news.

We were one hour late, and the ship for England had sailed.

We had only nine days left. We would never make it home in time!

As usual, Fogg was not worried. He simply went looking for a way to solve our problem.

And he found the *Henrietta.* She was a ship bound for France, carrying cloth and other goods.

"She is not a passenger ship!" said Andrew Speedy, her captain.

But Mr. Fogg gave him a lot of money. And soon, we were bound for Liverpool, England!

Mr. Fogg manned the wheel himself. We made good time until, a day out of Liverpool, we ran out of coal.

The ship slowed to a stop.

Mr. Fogg thought a second. Then he went to Captain Speedy.

"Would you sell me your ship?" he asked.

At first, the captain said no.

But then Mr. Fogg offered him most of the money in his bag.

Mr. Fogg called the crew together.

"I am now the owner of this ship," he said. "So go and get all of the wood you can find. We will use it as fuel in place of the coal. And when I say all the wood, I mean all the wood! Is that clear?"

"Orders are orders. If the captain wants wood, it's wood he'll have," said the oldest sailor on board. He began to remove a door from its hinges.

One by one, the cabins, masts, and fixtures were all burned. The whole ship was stripped to its shell.

It was just enough fuel to get us to Dublin, Ireland. We were near home!

We took a postal ship to Liverpool, England. We sat among the letters and packages.

When we reached Liverpool, it was noon on December 21st. We could get to London in less than six hours by train. It looked like we would win our bet!

Suddenly, Inspector Fix spoke up. "Mr. Phileas Fogg?" he said. "You're under arrest for the Bank of England robbery!"

"I am innocent!" Mr. Fogg said quietly.

But he was thrown in jail anyway.

We would never make it to the Reform Club in time!

Three hours later, Inspector Fix came back. "I'm terribly sorry," he said. "We just arrested the real thief. You are free to go."

We raced to the train station and boarded the first train to London.

But our train arrived in London five minutes too late.
We had lost the bet!

> *Have you ever lost after trying
> your best? How did you feel?*

We went home without saying a word.

I prepared a room for Aouda. Mr. Fogg stood in front of the fireplace, staring at the clock. I felt terrible. If I had told him who Fix was, perhaps things would have been different.

"I am so sorry," I said the next morning. "It is all my fault!"

But Mr. Fogg would not let me finish.

That evening, Mr. Fogg and Aouda talked for a long time.

And then Aouda asked Mr. Fogg to marry her.

And he accepted!

"Go to Reverend Wilson and ask him if he can marry us tomorrow, on Monday!" Mr. Fogg told me. I left for the reverend's house immediately.

I told the reverend that we wanted to reserve the church for the next day, Monday, December 23rd.

"Good," he said. "I am always happy to celebrate a wedding. But Monday the 23rd of December is not tomorrow; it is the day after tomorrow. Today is Saturday, December 21st."

And that's when I realized: because we had traveled from east to west around the world, and had crossed the International Date Line, we had actually gained a day. It was only Saturday!

I raced home to tell Mr. Fogg.

At precisely 8:45 that night, Mr. Phileas Fogg walked into the Reform Club.

He had won his bet.

He had traveled around the world in eighty days!

And on the next Monday, he and the Princess Aouda were married.

It was a wonderful ceremony... and a wonderful end to our adventure!

TREASURE ISLAND

Adapted from the story by Robert Louis Stevenson

My name is Jim Hawkins. At the time this story began, my father was the innkeeper at the *Admiral Benbow*, an inn in Bristol, England.

One day, a man came into the inn. He had a scar on his cheek. He had a rickety wheelbarrow. Inside it was a sailor's trunk.

He called himself Captain Bill. And he sang a pirate song: "Fifteen men on a dead man's chest. Yo ho ho and a bottle of rum!"

During the day, he would stand on the dock with his spyglass pointed out toward the sea.

At night, he would drink and drink and sing his pirate song. He was a strange man. Everyone was scared of him.

"Sing, you landlubbers!" he would cry, shaking his walking stick.

He was only afraid of one thing.

"If you see a sailor with only one leg, you must tell me, Jim!" he hissed.

I promised I would.

One day, a sailor *did* show up at the inn.

"I'm looking for my friend, Captain Bill," he said.

"He's out," I told him. "You'll have to wait."

When Captain Bill came back and saw the sailor, he grew pale.

"Do you remember me, Bill?" the sailor said. "Do you remember when we sailed under Captain Flint?"

"Black Dog!" gasped Captain Bill.

I heard them fighting from the next room and ran to get my father's friend, Doctor Livesey.

The two sailors had been on the same ship together. Why do you think they are fighting each other?

By the time we got back, Black Dog had run away and Captain Bill was lying on the ground.

"He has only fainted," Doctor Livesey told me. "We must carry him upstairs." And so we did.

"Black Dog!" gasped the Captain.

"There is no Black Dog here," the doctor told him.

But later, Captain Bill grabbed me by the collar.

"You must help me, boy!" he whispered. "I used to be a pirate. I have something in my sea chest that they want. You must tell me if any sailor comes back again! If not ..."

He stopped and looked around. "... they will give me the black spot!"

The black spot? What was that? I wondered.

Before I could find that out from Captain Bill, my father fell ill and, sadly, died soon after.

The day of my father's funeral, an old man came to the inn. He used a stick, and he had a blindfold over his eyes.

I thought he was helpless and frail. But he grabbed me by the arm and made me take him to Captain Bill.

There, he gave Captain Bill the black spot!

It was a piece of paper, condemning Captain Bill to death.

"We'll be back for ye tonight at ten," said the blind old man.

But Captain Bill did not last till ten. He fell dead of fright—right on the spot!

When I told my mother there were pirates coming to the inn, she took me to the village to ask for help.

But no one would help us.

"Pirates?" they all said. "Wewant nothing to do with pirates!"

What would you have done if you were a villager? Would you be scared of the pirates? Would you have helped Jim and his mother?

We soon were back at the inn.

"We must see what is in Captain Bill's trunk," my mother told me. "He owes us for his room. Perhaps there is something of value in there!"

There were only a few things in the trunk. We pulled out an old army uniform, some seashells, a coat, two brass compasses, a watch, and a leather bag.

But when my mother opened the bag... it was filled with gold!

There was also a strange package, rolled up in oilskin.

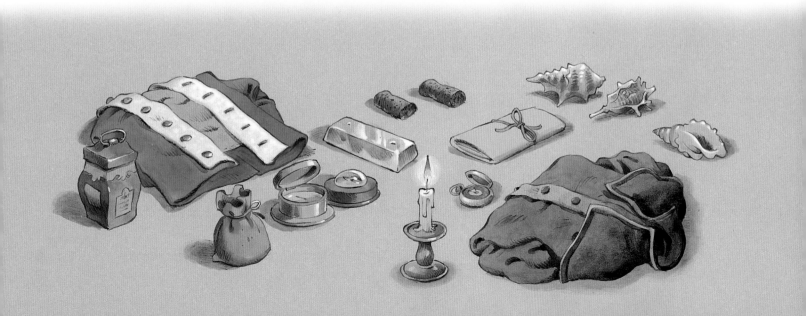

I took the package and hid it under my coat.

Then I heard a noise. It was the tap-tap-tapping cane of the blind man.

"The pirates!" I gasped. "Mother, we must hide!"

I put out the candle and we ran outside. There, we hid under a little stone bridge.

Soon, we could hear the pirates. There were seven or eight of them, led by the blind man.

"He's in there!" the blind man cried. "Break down the door!"

They were surprised to find the door open. But they were more suprised to find Bill dead.

"Get the trunk!" I heard the blind man say. But after a moment, he shouted again. "The map's not there!!!"

Just then, I heard hoofbeats.

It was a group of soldiers. They saved us from the pirates. Some of the pirates were captured, but a few escaped.

I knew there had to be something valuable in the package I had taken. So a solider and I took it to Doctor Livesey to show him.

Doctor Livesey was having dinner with Sir Trelawney. They both came out to see me.

"So, Jim. What is it?" Doctor Livesey asked.

I told him what had happened. Together we unwrapped the package.

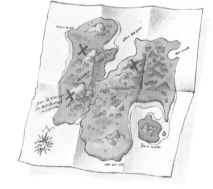

Inside was a book that showed how many ships Captain Flint and his pirate crew had sunk. And there was a map of an island... a map that showed the location of buried treasure!

"We must go find this treasure!" cried Sir Trelawney. "I will go to Bristol and find a ship and crew. Doctor, you must come with us. And you, too, Jim!"

And so I found myself embarking on a great adventure!

A week later, Sir Trelawney had indeed found a ship, the *Hispaniola*. He had also hired a crew.

"First I hired an old one-legged sailor named Long John Silver," he told us. "He will be our cook. Then *he* found the rest of the crew. They're all under Captain Smollet—a good man and an experienced seaman.

"Now run to the *Spyglass Inn*, Jim," he went on. "Find Long John and give him this letter from me."

But when I found Long John Silver, I also found someone else I knew.

"That's Black Dog!" I cried. "Stop him!"

"Take it easy, lad!" said Long John. "He's just an old sea dog. He won't hurt you."

Black Dog had disappeared. So I put him from my mind.

Finally, the moment I had been dreaming about arrived. We were on the *Hispaniola*, about to set sail!

"All the men suspect we are searching for treasure," Sir Trelawney told us. "We are in a dangerous position. I have locked up all the weapons. And whatever you do—make sure that no one sees the map!"

Then...
"Men, to your posts!" he cried. And we were underway!

Do you think Jim and his friends will find the treasure? Would you like to be with them on their adventure?

As the days went by, I found myself spending a lot of time with Long John. He knew everything about the sea. And he told many exciting stories about his adventures as we sat around the old wooden kitchen table.

One day I was hungry. So I climbed into the big apple barrel and ate three apples.

Then I fell asleep.

When I awoke, I heard some sailors talking.

I almost jumped out of the barrel. But then I heard Long John speak, and for a moment, I stopped breathing.

"Aye," he was saying. "We took many a ship's treasure when we were pirates working under Captain Flint. But no treasure, my lads, was as great as the treasure we are about to find!"

"Let's kill 'em all and take over the ship!" another voice said.

"Naw," said Long John slyly. "I have a better plan. We'll wait till we find the treasure. Then we'll rid ourselves of them all. Be patient, lads. Trust me!"

I was beginning to think I wouldn't make it out of the apple barrel alive. Then I heard someone call.

"Land ho! Land ho!"

All the sailors rushed out, and I climbed out of the barrel.

Then I ran out on deck and peered over the side. I could see a sliver of land in the distance.

Captain Smollet was talking to Long John Silver.

"You've sailed these waters, haven't you?" Smollet asked.

"Aye, Captain," said Long John Silver.

"Look at this map," Smollet said. "Is this Skeleton Island?"

Long John's eyes gleamed. I could tell he thought it was the treasure map!

But after he took the map, Long John's expression changed. It was only a copy. The places where the treasure was buried were not marked.

"Aye, Captain," Long John said. "This is that island."

When I could, I went to the captain's cabin with Doctor Livesey. Sir Trelawney and the captain himself were there, too.

I told them what I had heard from the apple barrel.

"Good boy, Jim!" said the doctor. "We must figure out a way to defend ourselves. In the meantime, keep an eye out. Tell us who is loyal, and who is a pirate."

 Jim is now a spy, isn't he? Would you like to have a spy adventure? What kind?

Skeleton Island was green and lush. And somewhere on it was buried treasure.

I couldn't wait to explore it!

We lowered two longboats into the sea.

Six sailors were staying aboard the ship. The captain, the doctor, and Sir Trelawney were going to the island. Thirteen sailors were going with them... and so was I.

I sneaked onto the second boat without anyone noticing me. Captain Smollet wanted me to spy on the pirates... so I did.

It was beautiful on the island, with strange birds and bright, colored flowers.

I climbed to the top of a hill to look around. But then I ducked down. I could hear Long John Silver!

He was trying to convince an old sailor named Tom to join him.

But when Tom said no, Long John threw his crutch at the man!

I was so afraid, I started to run!

Suddenly, I heard a noise. Then I saw a strange figure.

It was a man in tattered clothes. I had never seen him before.

"Stop!" I said, raising my arms. "Who are you?"

The man sank to his knees. "I'm Ben Gunn!" he said. "Happy to meet you."

"How did you get here?" I asked him.

"I was left here," he explained. "I was a pirate with Captain Flint. I knew about a treasure, and tried to take it for myself. So the captain left me here, all alone."

Ben Gunn has been on the island for a long time. What do you think it would be like to be alone on an island?

From out in the bay came the boom of a cannon. I started to run back to the beach.

On the way, I saw a fort. On it was a British flag.

Standing nearby was Doctor Livesey. He waved to me.

"Come on, Jim!" he called. "You must take shelter."

I was so glad to see him!

"What has happened?" I asked him.

"We went back to the ship to get more supplies," he told me. "But as we returned to shore, the pirates on the ship fired the cannon and sunk our longboat! They've taken over the ship!"

The fort was a log cabin surrounded by a fence. A spring of water ran nearby. As we raced inside, we were attacked by Long John and his men.

I was scared, but also excited. What an adventure!

Soon, we were all safely inside.

The next morning, we were awakened by a shout.

"White flag!" someone called. "We want to talk!"

When I ran out of the fort, I saw Long John Silver!

"If you give us the treasure map," he told the captain, "we'll let you live. We'll take you back on the ship and drop you at the nearest port. Or if you prefer, we'll leave you here with half the supplies. If not... you will die on Skeleton Island."

"I am still the captain of the ship," Smollett replied. "And I do not make deals with pirates!"

"You'll be sorry!" cried Long John Silver.

> _Would you have trusted Long John Silver?_
> _What would you have done?_

The next day, Long John came back with all the pirates.

"The battle is starting!" called Captain Smollet. "Everyone to your posts!"

There was much fighting. The smoke was thick.

But finally, we won.

However, the captain had been wounded.

"We cannot hold out here forever," said Doctor Livesey.

He sounded worried.

That's when I got an idea...

I knew how I could retake the *Hispaniola!*

While everyone was looking after the captain, I snuck out of the fort.

When I had roamed the island, I had noticed a small boat hidden in the reeds. I needed that boat to carry out my plan.

Finally, I found it!

Soon, I was paddling quickly and quietly toward the ship. When I got closer, I could see there were only two sailors on board. And they were fighting! My plan might work after all. I sat tight and waited...

When I climbed aboard early
the next morning, both sailors were
lying on deck.

One of them wasn't moving at all.

The other, I recognized. It was
Israel Hands.

Suddenly, Israel Hands jumped
up and started to chase me!

I climbed the mast, but he was
behind me.

Just as he was about to reach me, a gust of wind came up.

The boat rocked, and Hands fell into the sea!

I was now the captain of the *Hispaniola*! But there was no time to rejoice. I had to sail the ship around to the fort to rescue my friends.

It wasn't easy, but I did it. Then I left the ship and went to find my friends.

But when I got to the fort, I discovered Long John Silver and the pirates!

"We have reached an agreement with your friends," he told me. "They left us everything in return for their lives!"

"Let's get rid of the boy!" one of the pirates cried.

"No!" said Long John. "He will be our hostage!"

Later, Long John took me aside.

"Boy," he whispered, "you must trust me. I have made a deal with your friends. I'm going to help you. And in return, I get some of the treasure."

I didn't know if I should trust Long John or not. He had always been kind to me... but he was a pirate!

Doctor Livesey soon came to treat the wounded men. He had made an agreement with the pirates to do this.

I told him secretly about taking over the ship.

"You may have saved us again!" he whispered.

The next day, the pirates and I went off to find the treasure.

As we marched, we heard a strange voice, singing the old pirate song:

"Fifteen men on a dead man's chest. Yo ho ho and a bottle of rum!"

"It is the ghost of Captain Flint!" one of the pirates whispered.

We finally got to the place marked X on the map. But all that was there was a big, empty hole!

Long John moved near me. He handed me a gun. "Be ready to defend yourself!" he muttered.

At that moment, I heard shots. Three of the pirates fell.

It was the doctor and Sir Trelawney... and old Ben Gunn!

They quickly defeated the pirates and took Long John captive.

"Did you hear me singing?" Ben laughed. "I put fear in their black hearts, didn't I?"

"But where is the treasure?" I asked.

"Safe and sound!" said Doctor Livesey. "Ben helped us find it. And tomorrow, we will carry it to the ship... the ship you recaptured for us, Jim!"

I was very proud.

That night, we all camped in a cave on the beach.

The captain was feeling much better.

And there, in the corner, was the treasure! The gold gleamed in the light of the fire.

The next day, we rowed the treasure to the *Hispaniola*... and sailed home to England!

We decided to split the treasure. Soon after, Long John Silver disappeared with a *large* sack of gold coins.

"That old rascal!" the doctor said. "Well, good luck to him!"

I smiled.

I couldn't help but like Long John Silver... just a little. After all, it was partly due to him that I had had my great adventure of Treasure Island!

 *What do you think Jim will do with his part of the treasure? What would you do?*

THE LEGEND OF ROBIN HOOD

Adapted from the story by Howard Pyle

I am Sir Robert of Locksley, a noble knight born in a grand castle. This is my story.

At the end of the year 1100, a just and loved king, Richard the Lion Hearted, reigned in England. But soon, he left to join the Crusades.

He left his brother—Prince John—on the throne.

Prince John and his friends were evil men. One of his friends, the Sheriff of Nottingham, began to make the poor people of England pay enormous taxes. This left the people even poorer. They had barely enough food to feed themselves.

If you were a noble, you either agreed with Prince John or were against him. I made it clear I was for King Richard. So I lost my home and all my land.

That's when I began my life as an outlaw. I now steal from the rich and give to the poor.

Everyone calls me Robin Hood.

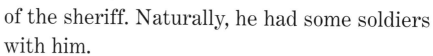

One morning, I was with a few friends when we saw Sir Guy of Gisborne, the cousin of the sheriff. Naturally, he had some soldiers with him.

"Seize Robin Hood!" shouted Sir Guy.

"Attack!" I cried, and immediately twenty arrows flew at Sir Guy and his henchmen. My arrow struck the helmet of Sir Guy, who fell down off his horse. (Not to brag, but I am famous for my aim.)

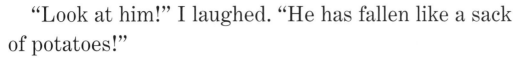

"Look at him!" I laughed. "He has fallen like a sack of potatoes!"

"I almost feel sorry for them," said my friend Gus.

It did not take much to convince Sir Guy's guards that it was better not to continue to fight. They went away with their tails between their legs, limping and full of bruises.

The day after, I saw a note pinned to a tree. It read: "Wanted! Five hundred gold pieces to whoever captures Robin Hood—dead or alive!"

It was clear I had to disappear for a little while. So I went to live deep in Sherwood Forest.

One day, as I traveled through Sherwood, I arrived at a river. There was a log that had fallen across it. The log acted as a kind of bridge.

I started across. But just then, I saw a large man begin to cross on the other side.

"Hey, little fellow!" he called to me. "Give way to Little John!"

"I started crossing first," I said. "You should give way to me!"

We both carried stout sticks of wood for balance. So when we got to the center of the log, we began to spar. Finally, I knocked him into the river.

"You are the first man ever to beat me— Little John," he said.

Why do you think such a big man was nicknamed Little John? Do you have a nickname?

That night, around the campfire, I told Little John my story. He decided to join us!

The next day, we met a fat friar.

"Your money or your life!" I told him.

"What money? I have no money," he answered.

"So then give me those barrels that you carry," I said. "What is inside?"

"Come and look, if you are brave enough!" he laughed, drawing a sword.

As we fought, he said, "Why do you steal from the people of the church?"

"I steal to help the poor!" I told him. "My name is Robin Hood!"

"I've heard of you, Robin!" the friar said, dropping his sword. "I am Friar Tuck. And I would like to join you!"

> *If you met Robin Hood, would you join his band? Why?*

In Sherwood Forest, we built shelters in the trees. We connected them with wooden bridges, and used ladders or ropes to climb down to the ground. We could protect ourselves more easily from up there.

We also had some secret trap doors leading to underground caves. This gave us other places to hide.

Each day, we would wait near the road to Nottingham.

If a poor person passed, we would give him a sack of money.

But when a noble friend of Prince John rode by, I would jump into the road and invite him to give us their gold.

They always said yes!

Why does Robin say that the nobles always say yes when he asks for their money?

One day, a cart passed through the forest.
With it were the personal guards of Prince John.
"That is an interesting cart," I told my men.
"I'll wager it carries a rich load of treasure!"

Little John stepped in front of the cart.

"Get out of the way, fat one!" sneered the driver.

"Are you calling me fat?" Little John shouted.
"I'll show you—"

And all by himself, he defeated the guards.
All we had to do was sit in our trees and watch!

"Bravo, Little John!" I cheered when the
frightened guards had escaped.

The cart was indeed filled with treasure. So the next day, I took it to the market and bought food. Then I gave the food to the people.

"Take these beautiful apples!" I told them. "Here is some bread! Meat, sugar, flour... it is all for you!"

We spent the entire day giving away our supplies.

"Thank you!" said one woman. "Now we have enough to feed our children! Thank you, Robin Hood!"

Do you think Robin Hood is trying to do good? Is there anyone in this story who might not think he's good? Why?

Later that day, we passed a working man in a cart.

"Hey, friend!" I said to him. "Where are you going?"

"To the market in Nottingham, to sell this meat," he said, showing me what was in his carriage.

Suddenly I had a great idea. "How much is your whole load worth, including the carriage?" I asked.

"Three gold pieces," he said.

"Here's seven. Now you can go back home," I told him, handing him a sack.

A little while later, I was at the market in Nottingham, selling the meat at very low prices. I even gave some of it away.

Some other merchants decided that I must be a rich person who wanted to help the poor.

"Why don't we invite him to the merchant's dinner?" said one. "He seems like a good fellow."

This fell right in with my plans. For the guest of honor at the dinner was none other than the Sheriff of Nottingham!

And so I went to the dinner. I actually sat next to the Sheriff!

He, too, thought I was rich. He never dreamed for an instant that I could be his worst enemy, Robin Hood!

"You know, I have a castle and a lot of land," I told him. "But I am bored with it. I would gladly give it all away."

"Dear me!" said the Sheriff greedily. "Don't give it away. I'll buy it from you. I can offer you 3,000 pounds. I have it right here in this bag!"

The property I had described was worth ten times what he was offering. But I pretended to accept.

"Let us go immediately to my castle," I told him.

We headed toward Sherwood Forest. The Sheriff rode on a beautiful horse. I rode in the butcher's wagon, pulled by a donkey.

You can imagine his surprise when he found himself surrounded by my men!

"What's happening?" he shouted.

"I think that money belongs to me!" I told him, taking the sack of gold.

"You'll pay for this," the Sheriff growled. "I'll have my revenge!"

Time went by. One day, a royal messenger went to Nottingham and all the nearby towns.

He announced an archery contest. It was open to all. It would be held at the castle of Prince John. And the prize for the best archer was a golden arrow.

Of course, I had to compete!

"Are you crazy?" shouted Will Scarlet. "Everyone knows you're the greatest archer in England. It's a trap!

The Sheriff will be there with all of his soldiers, just waiting to catch you!"

"I know," I told him. "But I can't resist."

My friends tried to talk me out of it. But they couldn't. So the day of the contest, we all dressed in disguises and went to the palace.

> *Why would Robin Hood go to the castle if he thinks he'll get caught?*

There were colored tents everywhere. A big crowd had gathered.

"Watch out!" Little John warned me. "The Sheriff's soldiers are all over."

"Don't worry!" I told him.

The contest began. I hit the bull's-eye every time. And soon, I had won the golden arrow!

"That archer is very good!" Prince John said, full of admiration.

He clearly hadn't recognized me!

"I don't know why," murmured Sir Guy of Gisborne, "but he reminds me of someone..."

Do you think Sir Guy of Gisborne will recognize Robin Hood? Why does Robin look familiar to him?

"As soon as I accept my reward, we'll disappear," I told my friends.

Little John shook his head. "I'm coming with you," he decided.

We walked over to the stands.

"I congratulate you," Prince John began.

Suddenly, Sir Guy jumped to his feet.

"I know you!" he cried. "You're Robin Hood!" And he yanked off my hat and wig.

"Quick, get him!" the Sheriff of Nottingham cried.

In a flash, the guards surrounded us. But we were faster. We hopped on our horses and raced to Sherwood Forest!

That same day, I found out that Lady Marian, King Richard's cousin, had returned from London. She had been living there for several years.

I had known Lady Marian when I lived in a castle. I liked her very much. And I knew she would try to help us... and her cousin, the King.

That evening, we went to see her.

"I have heard much of you while I was away," Marian told me. "The famous Robin Hood is known throughout the land.

"Sir Guy of Gisborne's soldiers were here earlier," she added. "They were looking for treasure. The Sheriff is a greedy man."

"Can you help us?" I asked. "We need to tell King Richard what is going on."

"Of course!" said Marian. "I have written a letter to him. My governess, Rebecca, will deliver it. Rebecca, are you ready?"

"Certainly, madam!" Rebecca said. "I'll leave right away!"

But no sooner had Rebecca gone than she was arrested by the Sheriff's men.

There were spies everywhere!

How do you think the Sheriff knew that Rebecca had the letter?

That same night, Sir Guy of Gisborne and his soldiers knocked again at Lady Marian's castle.

"You are under arrest," said Sir Guy. "You are coming with us."

"What is the charge?" Lady Marian demanded.

"We caught your servant with a letter to King Richard," replied Sir Guy.

Marian was forced to go with him.

I was in the forest when Will Scarlet, one of my men, came running up to me.

"Robin!" he shouted. "They've arrested Lady Marian!"

"We must save her before she leaves the forest!" I said.

Little John came up with a plan. We galloped ahead of Lady Marian and the soldiers.

Then we cut down an old oak tree to block the road.

When Sir Guy and the soldiers arrived with Lady Marian, we sprang upon them.

Soon, we overpowered them.

I myself knocked Sir Guy off his horse.

"I beg you, Robin, spare my life!" the villain pleaded.

"Leave, then, and take your soldiers with you!" I told him.

"Thanks to all of you for saving me," Marian said.
Looking me in the eyes, she whispered, "And above all,
thanks to you, Robin!"

I knelt before her. "I would do anything to help you,
Marian," I said.

"And I still need help," she told me. "I cannot go home
again. May I come and join you in Sherwood Forest?"

"Of course!" I said.

Marian adjusted to life in the forest right away. It was nice to have her there. Everyone liked her.

Early one morning, Little John woke me.

"Robin! A group of the Sheriff's soldiers are approaching the forest."

I got up immediately.

"Send the men to their posts," I said.

I could hear the sound of horses and men.
Soon, I could see them, too. There seemed to be hundreds of them.

Oh, no! Sherwood Forest is being attacked.
What do you think will happen to Robin Hood?

We fought as best we could. But we were outnumbered.

Suddenly, some archers began shooting flaming arrows at our homes.

Before long, the forest was burning! Many of our people were captured... including Lady Marian.

"We must escape while we can, Robin!" Will Scarlet said.

I hated to give up, but I knew he was right.

"If we are free, we can help our friends," I told my men. "For now, we must disappear."

All of us were sad. But there was no choice.

The Sheriff's men had destroyed our homes in Sherwood Forest. But we had other things to worry about.

We had sent Friar Tuck to the Nottingham Castle to see what the Sheriff was plotting.

When he returned, he had terrible news.

"They are building a scaffold in the castle courtyard," he told me. "The Sheriff wants to hang four of our men!"

"When?" I asked him.

"Tomorrow," he told me. "And there's more. After the execution, the Sheriff is planning a wedding."

"For whom?" I asked. I was afraid I already knew the answer.

"For *him*—and Lady Marian!" he told me.

"What are we to do?" inquired Will Scarlet.

"We'll rescue them, of course!" I said.

The next day we dressed up as beggars and blended into the crowd in front of the scaffold. We had disguised ourselves well. No one knew we were there.

There was a drum roll. Then the executioner put the ropes around our dear friends' necks.

That's when Little John jumped up onto the scaffold. With all his strength, he started tugging on it until it fell.

We threw off our disguises and started to fight the soldiers.

Little John shouted, "People of Nottingham, fight with us against the Sheriff! For Robin Hood! For freedom! For King Richard!"

His words encouraged the people to act. Everyone joined in the fight.

I looked around for the Sheriff. That's when I saw him runnning into a tower taking Marian with him.

"Robin, help me!" she cried.

I started after them. "I'm coming, Marian!" I called.

Will Robin rescue the Lady Marian? What do you think?

I ran to the top of the tower.
The Sheriff was waiting.

"Take care, Robin!" Marian cried.

We fought for a long time. The
Sheriff was better with the sword
than I had excepted.

But finally, he slipped and rolled down the stairs.

"Robin!" Marian said. "We must escape before someone
else comes."

At that moment, we heard
a voice.

"Who's there?" I asked.

"The cook... I'm a loyal subject
of King Richard," the voice said.
"I know a tunnel. Follow me!"

"Marian, you must go with
him," I said. "I have to help my
friends. Then I'll join you."

"No," she said.
"I'll wait for you here."

I found many of my friends

fighting in the courtyard.

"Follow me!" I called.

We raced to the front hall of the castle.

Then I grabbed my ax and broke the chain that held the door open.

The door slammed shut—leaving the Sheriff's men on the other side!

My men and I raced back to the tunnel.

"Welcome!" Marian greeted us with a smile.

Soon we found ourselves far away from the castle.

"We made it!" Little John exclaimed.

"Thank you, Robin, for rescuing me," Lady Marian said sincerely.

We returned to the forest, built new homes, and went back to our lives as outlaws.

We continued to rob from the rich to give to the poor. In the meantime, we prayed for King Richard to return and restore peace and justice to the land.

What we didn't know was that he was closer than we thought.

Disguised as friars, the King and his friend, Sir Hurbert, were riding along the path that crossed Sherwood Forest. They were looking for us!

One day, Little John, Will Scarlet, and I met up with two hooded men. They were carrying sacks of gold.

"Your money, good sirs!" I said, stepping out in front of them. "The poor will thank you for your charity!"

"And who are you?" the taller stranger asked.

"They call me Robin Hood," I told him.

"Then bow to your King," he said, taking off his hood.

It was King Richard. He was home again!

Peace and justice were soon restored to England. Each of us returned to our homes. And Lady Marian and I were married.

It was truly a happy ending for us all!

20,000 LEAGUES UNDER THE SEA

Adapted from the story by Jules Verne

This is a sea story, but not just any sea story. This is a story with whales and giant squids, brave sailors and fantastic worlds under the ocean.

It is a strange story, but a true one. I know because it happened to me, Professor Peter Aronnax, of the Museum of Natural History in Paris.

It all began in New York. I had just returned from a long expedition with my faithful assistant, Conseil.

That was when I first heard of the sea monster. There were rumors about it all over the city. The Americans were organizing an expedition to try to find it. I was hoping they'd ask me to go.

Finally, they did. The invitation came from the Secretary of the United States Marines.

We would be traveling on the vessel, the *Abraham Lincoln*.
Our captain would be Commander Farragut.

"Conseil?" I called. "We are going in search of a giant sea monster!"

"I will pack our bags," said Conseil.

The sailors of the *Abraham Lincoln* were busy getting ready to sail.

We soon met Commander Farragut.

As we were boarding the ship, I felt someone put his hand on my shoulder.

"Holy Smoke! You're Professor Aronnax, the sea monster expert," he said. "I'm Ned Land, the harpooner. I'm sailing with you. Pleased to meet you."

"The pleasure is mine," I responded, rubbing my shoulder. He was a strong young man!

I introduced Mr. Land to Conseil. And then we boarded the boat.

We were on our way!

Can you guess why Commander Farragut would want a harpooner on the trip to find the sea monster?

We started our trip hoping that we would soon find the monster. But after weeks on the open seas, the only thing we had seen was water.

Ned and I had become friends. He passed his time in the crow's nest, looking for the sea monster. I spent my days on deck, doing the same.

One day, we both saw something.

It was gray and shiny, and it was headed right toward us!

Ned grasped his harpoon. "I'm ready for you, sea monster!" he cried.

Commander Farragut had his men load the cannon.

"Be ready to fire as soon as it's within range!" he ordered.

The monster got closer and closer. Ned aimed his harpoon.

Suddenly, I noticed something strange.

"That's not right!" I cried.

But no one paid any attention to me.

"Fire!" cried Farragut.

There was a great "Boom!" The ship shook and the air was filled with smoke. I couldn't see the monster anywhere.

"Hooray! We did it!" cried the crew.

"Something is wrong," I insisted, looking over the rail. "I am sure that the monster had lights inside it! And that someone turned off those lights—"

Without warning, the creature rammed our ship!

In an instant, I went flying into the sea!

When I rose to the surface, Conseil was in the water, too. So was Ned!

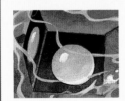

What do you think Aronnax was talking about? What was "wrong" with the monster?

The "sea monster" rose up right underneath us!

"Touch it!" Ned said, surprised. "It feels like metal!" It did, indeed.

At that moment, a hatch in the "monster" opened. Some sailors climbed out. Then they dragged us inside!

What do you think the sea monster really is?

We soon found ourselves in a small, dark room.

"I can't see a thing!" I told my friends. I was wet and cold and getting a little annoyed.

"Ouch! I can tell you that there's a wall here," complained Ned. "And it's pretty hard!"

"I'm quite hungry," Conseil noted.

At that moment, we heard a door open. Then, someone turned on a light.

"Gentlemen, dinner is served," a sailor said. "And here are some freshly pressed clothes."

Before we could say anything, the sailors disappeared.

"What are we to do?" I wondered.

"I think we should change and eat," said the sensible Conseil.

And so we did.

Then we took a nap.

A sailor woke us.

Ned immediately jumped up, grabbing him by the neck.

"Where are we? Why have you locked us up in here?" Ned demanded. "And where is the captain?"

"I," exclaimed a deep voice, "am Captain Nemo."

We turned.

"You are on the *Nautilus*, my submarine," the captain went on. "I have prepared some cabins for you. Please come with me."

We were so surprised that we couldn't say a word. We simply followed him.

Soon after, I found myself in an elegant dining room with Captain Nemo.

"Your library is quite large," I said.

"This is only a small part of my library," Nemo explained.

"The rest is in my home."

"I wish I had the time to read all these books," I said politely.

"You'll have all the time you want," Nemo said. "You and your companions must remain here forever."

I was amazed. "And why is that?" I asked.

"You already know too much," he said. "I must protect the *Nautilus*."

I told this all to Conseil and Ned when we met later that night. We had no intention of staying on the *Nautilus*. We had to find a way to escape!

THE
Nautilus

COMPARTMENT
CONTAINING T[
ROWBOAT

COMMAND POST

OBSERVATION
DECK

RECEPTION
HALL

NEMO'S
ROOM

3850

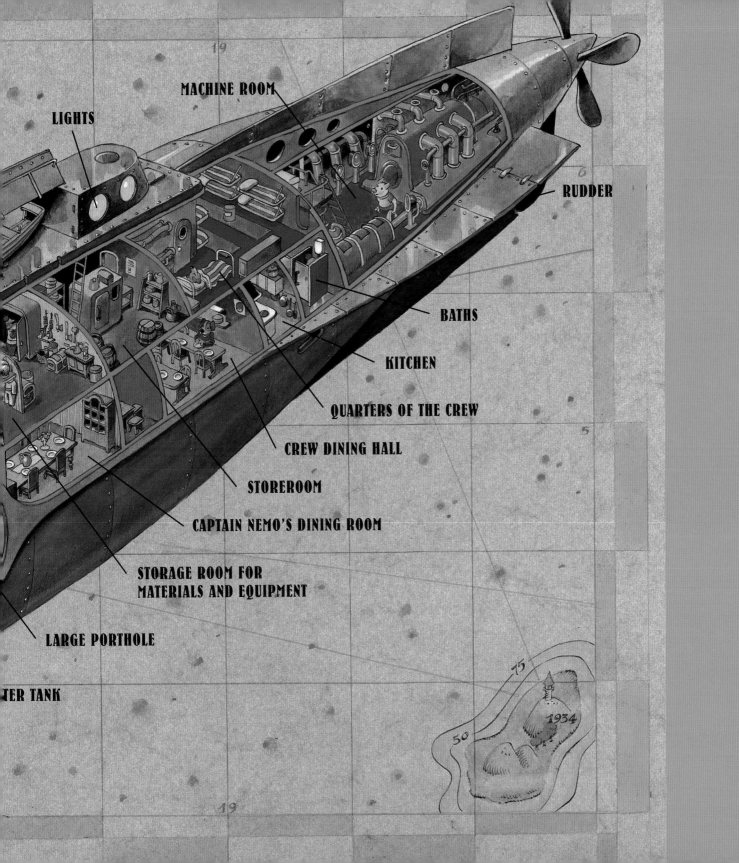

MACHINE ROOM

LIGHTS

RUDDER

BATHS

KITCHEN

QUARTERS OF THE CREW

CREW DINING HALL

STOREROOM

CAPTAIN NEMO'S DINING ROOM

STORAGE ROOM FOR
MATERIALS AND EQUIPMENT

LARGE PORTHOLE

TER TANK

50

75

1934

19

The next day, Ned, Conseil, and I watched the sea through the *Nautilus'* great porthole.

"How amazing!" I said.

"Why don't we go outside?" Captain Nemo suggested.

"Can we?" I asked.

"Of course!" said Nemo.

Soon we were supplied with diving suits with speaker systems, oxygen tanks, and flashlights. Then we took our first walk on the bottom of the ocean. Even Conseil was amazed.

Suddenly, Nemo pushed me to the ground.

Then he shot a spear at a giant spider that was about to attack me.

"Thank you, Captain," I said.

Nemo called out, "To the ground!"

We all got down. Within an instant, two giant, hungry-looking sharks were swimming above us.

"You have saved me two times," I told the captain gratefully. "I thank you."

Back aboard the *Nautilus*, our travels continued until we became stuck on a barrier reef. The reef was just off a lush and beautiful island.

"When the high tide arrives, we'll be able to leave," Nemo told us.

"May we visit the island?" I asked.

"Go on," the captain said. He knew we could not escape.

The island was full of beautiful animals and bright green plants.

We watched as some brilliantly-colored birds flew above our heads.

We had rifles with us for protection. But I hated hunting. We would never have hurt any of the animals on the island.

Suddenly, a group of savage-looking men came out of the bushes. They were headed toward us!

We raced to the beach and rowed back to the *Nautilus* just in time. But the men followed us.

I rushed into the hall to inform Captain Nemo.

"We are under attack!" I cried.

But the captain stayed completely calm.

"There is no need for concern," Nemo told me. "Our attackers will never be able to get inside. The outside of the *Nautilus* is secure. It is also wired with electricity. If anyone tries to come on board, they will receive a nasty shock. Soon, they will give up."

Captain Nemo was right. They soon did.

When the tide rose, we got underway again.
We traveled night and day.
One morning, Captain Nemo approached us.
"Would you like to go pearl diving?" he asked.
"Of course!" said Ned enthusiastically.

We took the boat.
It was loaded with our
gear. We were soon at
the Bay of Giant Pearls.
There, we put on
our diving suits and
jumped into the water.

The captain led us to a secret cave. In a corner was an oyster larger than any other. Nemo opened its shell, revealing the biggest pearl I had ever seen.

"What do you think of this little jewel?" he asked.

"Amazing!" said Ned, astonished.

The captain did not pick up the pearl. Instead, he gently closed the oyster shell.

"Why didn't you take it?" asked Ned.

"Each time I come to see it, it is larger and more beautiful," Nemo explained. "I'm not interested in owning it. I just like to look at it now and then."

I had to admit that I was impressed. Captain Nemo was clearly not a greedy man.

There were many island native pearl divers all around us. One had a rock tied to his ankle.

"The weight helps him get to the bottom quickly," Nemo told us. "That way, he will have more time to search for pearls before he runs out of air."

Just then, a shark attacked the defenseless man.

"We must help him!" cried Nemo. Without thinking of his own safety, he quickly rushed at the shark. He pulled, poked, and punched.

Ned joined in to help, poking the shark with his harpoon. Finally, the shark swam off.

In the meantime, Conseil had rushed over to help the pearl diver. He quickly took the man to the surface so he could breathe.

Later, Captain Nemo gave the man a sack of beautiful pearls.

"He is poor," Nemo explained. "Helping him is the right thing to do."

I was confused. The captain was a strange man. On the one hand, he seemed very hard. But he was also sensitive and generous.

Soon, we were underway again.

One day, Captain Nemo sent for me. I joined him by the giant porthole.

I gasped. Before me was a sunken ship. Around it were divers. They were filling large baskets with the gold and jewels that the ship had carried.

"This is why I am wealthy," Nemo explained. "I hunt for sunken treasure. There are so many ships that lie at the bottom of the sea. And with the *Nautilus*, I can find them all!

"And there are other treasures under the sea," Nemo went on. "May I show them to you?"

"Of course!" I exclaimed.

What else might you find on a sunken ship?

A few hours later, Captain Nemo and I were walking through an underwater city.

I gasped. "Could this be... the lost city of Atlantis?" I cried.

It was truly an extraordinary sight—a city at the bottom of the ocean.

We went back to the submarine. Soon, we found ourselves inside an extinct volcano. Captain Nemo had stopped there to refuel. The volcano was full of coal.

This seemed to be a good time to try to escape.

So Conseil, Ned, and I sneaked out of the *Nautilus* and tired to climb up the volcano's walls.

We struggled hard. But the walls were too steep, and we were forced to return to the submarine. Nemo said nothing about it.

Can you think of any other ways for Aronnax, Conseil, and Ned to escape? Would you want to escape?

"Our next destination is the South Pole," Nemo told me.

"Don't be silly!" I told him. "No one has ever dared such a thing!"

"We will!" the captain said.

After many days under water, the *Nautilus* tried to rise to the surface.

It was difficult. There was a thick sheet of ice above us.

But we finally got through!

By moving slowly, we broke the ice in front of us, too. Finally, we arrived at Nemo's destination—the South Pole!

Nemo invited us to leave the ship with him. He was headed to the heart of the South Pole.

"This is the chance of a lifetime!" I said. "I would be honored to go with you."

Ned didn't want to join us. But Conseil did.

The three of us walked to the Pole. There, Captain Nemo planted his flag.

Perhaps it is still there today!

What would you leave at the South Pole?

We soon were underway again. But our journey was short. We had become trapped below the ice.

Nemo and some of the crew went out to cut the submarine free.

In the meantime, we waited inside.

It was getting difficult to breathe in the thin air. At some point, I fainted.

———◇———

When I came to, I was wearing an oxygen mask.

The crew had managed to free the *Nautilus*, and we were rising to the surface.

We could all breathe easily now.

After our trip to the South Pole, we headed north, past South America.

One day, Conseil and I were at the great porthole with Captain Nemo when I saw something impossible.

"They look like squid," said Conseil.

"But they are giants!" I cried.

"Giant squid, to be exact," noted my faithful assistant.

"They do appear to be so," said Nemo.

Suddenly, a sailor burst into the room. "A squid is wrapping itself around the ship! What do we do?"

"Quick. We must dive immediately!" Nemo ordered.

Then he grabbed an ax and ran to the main hatch.

"I'll get my harpoon," cried Ned.

We went out onto the hull of the *Nautilus*. The squid was trying to crush the submarine.

"Take this!" said Nemo.

"And this!" Conseil and I added.

We hit the tentacles of the monster with our axes.

Nearby, a sailor had been picked up by the squid. He surely would have perished, but Nemo saved him.

A moment later, it was Ned himself who was in the squid's grasp!

But again, Captain Nemo came to the rescue.

The squid then vanished beneath the sea.

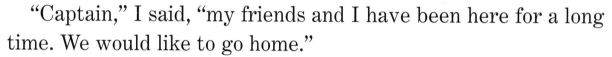

That evening, I joined Nemo in his study.

"Captain," I said, "my friends and I have been here for a long time. We would like to go home."

Captain Nemo stared at me. "I told you before," he said. "You and your friends must remain here forever!"

I could not understand Captain Nemo. He would risk his life to save us… and yet we were his prisoners.

What do you think of Captain Nemo? Will Aronnax and his friends ever get to go home?

The *Nautilus* headed for Europe. One night, a ship appeared. It looked like a battle ship. Its cannons were pointed at us—and it began to fire straight at our submarine!

"So they want to sink us, do they?" cried Nemo. "Then we'll give them just the same treatment!"

He ordered the lights turned off. Then he rammed the large battle ship, shattering it!

That night, Conseil, Ned, and I met in my cabin.

"We must escape!" Ned whispered.

"But how?" Conseil asked.

"We will steal a rowboat," I decided. "With the remains of the ship all around us, perhaps we will not be noticed."

I saw Captain Nemo one more time that night. He was calmly playing the organ.

I was never to see him again.

We were already on board the rowboat when we heard a cry rising from the *Nautilus*.

"Maelstrom! Maelstrom!"

A maelstrom is a giant whirlpool of water that sucks up everything in its path. It grabbed hold of the *Nautilus* and dragged it to the bottom of the sea.

Luckily, we were thrown far away by giant waves. A fisherman finally picked us up. He fed us hot soup in his small cabin.

And that is how we escaped from the *Nautilus* and Captain Nemo.

Perhaps Nemo survived. Perhaps he is out there today, visiting the giant pearl, battling giant squid and dangerous sharks.

But we will never know…

Do you think the Nautilus *and its crew survived?*

KING ARTHUR AND THE KNIGHTS OF THE ROUND TABLE

My name is Merlin. I am the most famous magician who ever lived. I'm going to tell you a story that took place in England long ago… so long ago that even I cannot remember when it happened…

It all began when my grandfather gave me his magic powers. These, added to my own, made me very powerful indeed.

There was a battle with dragons, too, but that's another story.

This story begins when I became the personal advisor of King Uther Pendragon of Camelot.

One night, I had a dream that the king would soon die and that the king's newborn son would be in danger. So I made a pact with King Uther. I would take the child away from Camelot and protect and educate him until he became king. He was to be the greatest king that England had ever known!

The child's name was Arthur.

I gave Arthur to a friend of mine, Sir Hector. I did not tell him who Arthur was. But Hector was a good man and asked no questions. He treated Arthur like one of his own sons.

Soon after that, King Uther Pendragon died.

Eighteen years later, Hector's oldest son, Kay, was training to be a knight. Arthur wanted to be one, too. But in the meantime, he was acting as Kay's squire.

It was the time of the great Christmas tournament in Camelot. Kay was going to compete. Arthur went with him.

But Kay had forgotten his sword. He sent Arthur back to get it.

It was quite late, and Arthur was worried that he wouldn't return with the sword in time. In the middle of a square, he saw a big stone with an anvil on top. Stuck in the anvil was a sparkling sword.

Arthur went over to it. "I'll just borrow this sword," he thought. "I'll return it after the tournament is over."

When Arthur came back and gave the sword to Kay, Hector gasped. "That is Excalibur, the magic sword! Arthur, how did you get it?"

Arthur hadn't noticed the writing on the anvil. It said, "*Whoever succeeds in drawing this sword from the stone will become King of England.*"

The knights all laughed, "Arthur, King of England? It cannot be! If he really pulled the sword from the anvil, let him put it back and do it again!"

And so Arthur put the sword back. The strongest knights tried to pull the sword from the stone, but they failed.

Finally, Arthur easily drew the sword from the stone again. Now everyone was convinced. "Long live the King!" they cried.

That same evening Arthur was crowned King of England in the castle of Camelot, fulfilling his destiny. Though he was young, Arthur proved to be a wise and generous king.

One day, he heard that one of his subjects, Leodagan of Carmelide, was being attacked by an evil king from the north, so he led his armies to help Leodagan.

The battle was fierce. But King Arthur managed to drive off the invaders.

From the castle walls, a young woman watched. She was Leodagan's beautiful daughter, Guinevere.

When the fighting was done, Leodagan invited Arthur to a big banquet to celebrate. There, Arthur met Guinevere.

During the banquet, Arthur and Guinevere looked into each other's eyes. They hardly ate a thing.

"It seems that the young king has found his queen!" I thought.

And I was right. Soon after, Arthur asked Guinevere to marry him. And she accepted.

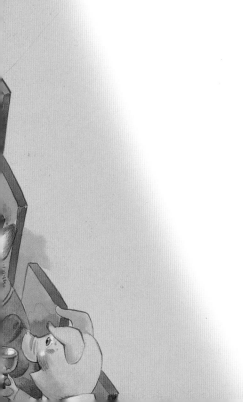

I wondered what to get Arthur and Guinevere for a wedding gift. But one night, a fairy appeared to me. She told me of an old prophesy:

Arthur and all his knights would sit at a round table, she said. All the knights would be equal. All would help one another.

So I gave Arthur a giant round table. On each chair was written the name of one of his knights.

The following day, Arthur summoned to court the knights whose names appeared on the chairs.

"Sit with us!" said Arthur. Then, in a solemn tone, he proclaimed, "There are still many empty chairs, but I know that destiny will bring us the missing knights. I declare the first session of the Knights of the Round Table—OPEN!"

Now that Arthur was safely on the throne, I could go back to my magic potions.

One day, I heard of a young man named Lancelot. He was the son of a king, but he had been orphaned. He was raised by the magical Viviane,

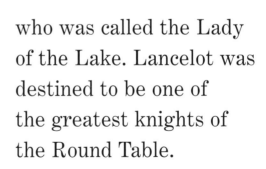

who was called the Lady of the Lake. Lancelot was destined to be one of the greatest knights of the Round Table.

Viviane was even more powerful than I. She lived in a castle under the lake. She had given England the great sword, Excalibur. And some day, it would return to her.

It came to pass that Viviane and Lancelot left the magic castle under the lake. They were headed for King Arthur's castle.

The Lady of the Lake had given Lancelot a white suit of armor and a magnificent white horse.

Viviane rode out in front. Behind her was Lancelot, handsome and proud. Soldiers and servants followed them, carrying gifts for the king.

Everyone who saw this parade of beauty and strength was impressed.

When Viviane and Lancelot reached Camelot, Viviane said to King Aurthur, "Sire, this courageous youth has come to take his place among the knights. His name is Lancelot du Lake."

Arthur was happy to welcome Lancelot. The young man soon sat at the round table.

Later, Sir Lancelot met Guinevere.

"My Queen," he said, kneeling. "I will be proud to fight in your name."

"And I am proud to know such a heroic knight fights for me!" she said.

At that moment, a great friendship was born between Lancelot and Queen Guinevere.

When Lancelot left for his first mission, he carried with him a magnificent silver sword. It was a gift from Guinevere.

As he rode across the country, he saw a man dressed in black who rode a black horse.

"I am the Black Knight, and I order you to leave here now!" he said.

Lancelot drew his new sword and challenged the knight. He was winning the duel when a storm of angry birds threw themselves against him.

Lancelot started to attack the birds. But the Black Knight stopped him.

"Do not harm them!" he cried. "A spell has transformed all the women in my castle into these birds. In a few days, they will become women again. If you have a good heart, please go away and leave us in peace."

Lancelot, of course, agreed.

One day, a beautiful woman came to the court of King Arthur. She looked exactly like Queen Guinevere!

"I am the true Guinevere!" she claimed. "This other one kidnapped me when I was coming to my wedding.

The other Guinevere protested.

"Arthur, she is lying!" she said. "She is a witch! I am your true wife!"

But Arthur had already fallen under the witch's spell. For indeed, the false Guinevere was a powerful witch!

Just then, Lancelot rushed in. Not being under the spell, he could tell the true Guinevere from the false one.

"This is the true Guinevere!" shouted Arthur, pointing to the witch.

"It is not!" Lancelot shouted back. "And whoever says it is must fight me!"

The code of knighthood decreed that it was possible to determine who was telling the truth by fighting. Whoever was innocent would win.

And so Lancelot faced every knight who defended the false queen—and knocked them all down, one by one.

When the last challenger had fallen, Lancelot turned to the false queen.

"Disappear!" he shouted. "Forever!"

And as if by magic—and in fact, it was—the strange queen suddenly vanished.

Guinevere was furious with everyone, especially Arthur. None of them had believed her. She decided to leave Camelot forever. But Lancelot begged her to stay.

"Everyone needs you," he told her. "Especially King Arthur. He is a better king when you are by his side."

Guinevere finally nodded. "You were the only one who believed in me!" she told Lancelot. "So for you, I will stay. Take this ring. It is a sign of my gratitude and my affection."

"Thank you, My Lady!" Lancelot said.

And so Guinevere returned to her place on the throne.

 Guinevere was really angry. Do you ever get angry? How does it feel?

The Knights of the Round Table liked to take long horseback rides in the woods.

It was during one of these that Gawain, a brave knight and friend of Sir Lancelot, was kidnapped by a giant.

"I must go and look for my friend," Lancelot decided.

A peasant woman told Lancelot that Gawain had been kidnapped by Caradoc. Caradoc lived in the Land of Sorrow.

"To get there," the woman told him, "you must cross the Valley of No Return. That is the valley that belongs to the evil witch, Morgan le Fay. Only a pure heart can cross that place!"

"Thank you," Lancelot told her. "I am not afraid!"

When Lancelot reached the valley, he saw a cloud of smoke. Suddenly, four giant dragons appeared, spitting fire from their nostrils. Lancelot got off his horse, drew his sword and killed them in an instant.

Next, three tall knights appeared to fight him. Lancelot defeated them, too.

"Ah, my favorite dragons! And my knights!" shouted Morgan le Fay. She used her powerful magic, and Lancelot quickly fell into a deep sleep. When he awoke, Morgan was in front of him.

"I must free Gawain!" were the first words of the brave knight.

"You may go free him," said Morgan le Fay. "But only if you promise to return to me."

"I promise," said Sir Lancelot. And because Morgan knew that he would keep his word, she let him go.

Lancelot found Gawain in a terrible prison. Guarding it was the giant, Caradoc.

Lancelot defeated the giant and freed his friend.

If you were Lancelot, would you keep your promise to return to Morgan le Fay? Why?

Lancelot and Gawain feasted all night. But when Gawain fell asleep, Lancelot quietly went off and returned to Morgan le Fay. He had given her his word, and he could not do otherwise.

He was exhausted, and he soon fell asleep.

While he slept, the evil Morgan sent a letter to King Arthur that said:

"From this moment I am no longer a part of the Round Table. Goodbye.

Signed, Lancelot du Lake."

When Arthur read it to the knights, everyone despaired. But Guinevere didn't believe it.

And neither did Gawain.

The next day, a strange knight came to Camelot. He challenged one of the Knights of the Round Table to a duel.

"The Queen must join us," the Knight said. "She will stay in the forest so that everything goes according to plan."

King Arthur thought this was dangerous to do. But in those times, you couldn't refuse a challenge to a duel. So the king accepted. And Sir Kay volunteered to fight for the queen.

But Sir Kay returned home without the queen. The whole thing had been a trick. The queen had been kidnapped!

Gawain set out, determined to find both Guinevere and Sir Lancelot. On the way, he met a fellow dragging a cart. On the cart was a mysterious figure wrapped in a dark cape.

"You are looking for Guinevere," the figure said. "Follow me and you will discover where they are holding her prisoner."

The figure reminded Gawain of someone. But he followed in silence.

Finally, the strange group reached a castle. Gawain asked the lady of the place to take them in.

"I must leave," said the driver of the cart. "But I can tell you now that Guinevere is at Gorre's castle."

At that point, the other man took off his heavy cape.

 It was Lancelot!

Gawain was happy to see his friend. "But where have you been?" he asked.

"I was imprisoned by Morgan le Fay," Lancelot explained. "But my mother, Viviane, freed me. I was headed to Camelot when I heard of Guinevere's fate. My mother advised me to disguise myself, which worked well—yes, my friend? But, we *must* go now to Gorre's castle. Do you know how to find it?'

"Yes, my friend," said Gawain. "It is at the top of a very tall mountain. But that's not all. There are only two entrances. One is deep under water. The other is across a metal bridge that is sharper than a sword. And guarding every door are three knights with extraordinary strength."

"Whose castle is it?" Lancelot asked.

"The good king Gorre," Gawain replied. "The problem is not him, but his evil son, Meleagant. It was he who must have taken the queen hostage."

The two knights soon reached Gorre's castle. "I will take the bridge," said Sir Lancelot. "You will go under the water."

Then he tied bandages around his hands so he wouldn't cut himself as he crossed the bridge. Guinevere watched from the tower above, concerned for her friend.

Lancelot is brave, isn't he? When was a time when you have been brave?

As soon as Lancelot was inside the castle, the evil Meleagant challenged him to a duel. But the duel was brief. Meleagant lay on the ground, begging for mercy.

"Save him!" said Guinevere. "King Gorre is wise. He will punish his son and put him back on the right path."

Just then, Gawain entered. He was soaking wet.

"What a shame!" he said. "I'm late for the duel!"

"But you're in time for our return to Camelot!" said Sir Lancelot with a smile.

They returned that very day. King Arthur was grateful to get his queen and his two loyal knights back again.

I, Merlin, could easily hear the sounds of their laughter and cheers, even from many miles away.

After all, I am the greatest magician who ever lived!